P9-DVA-848

CHILDREN'S THRIFT CLASSICS

The Call of the Wild

JACK LONDON

Adapted by Bob Blaisdell
Illustrated by John Green

DOVER PUBLICATIONS, INC.
Mineola, New York

DOVER CHILDREN'S THRIFT CLASSICS
Editor of This Volume: Jill Jarnow

Bibliographical Note

This Dover edition, first published in 1999, is a new abridgment of a standard text of *Call of the Wild*. The introductory Note and the illustrations were prepared specially for this edition.

Library of Congress Cataloging-in-Publication Data

Blaisdell, Robert.
    The call of the wild / by Jack London ; adapted by Bob Blaisdell ; illustrated by John Green.
        p.   cm. — (Dover children's thrift classics)
    Summary: The adventures of an unusual dog, part St. Bernard, part Scotch shepherd, that is forcibly taken to the Klondike gold fields where he eventually becomes the leader of a wolf pack.
    ISBN-13: 978-0-486-40551-3 (pbk.)
    ISBN-10: 0-486-40551-6 (pbk.)
    1. Dogs—Juvenile fiction. [1. Dogs—Fiction. 2. Wolves—Fiction. 3. Yukon Territory—Fiction.] I. London, Jack, 1876–1916. II. Green, John, ill. III. Title. IV. Series.
PZ7.B545Ca1   1999
[Fic]—dc21   98–49244
                                                                                      CIP
                                                                                      AC

Manufactured in the United States by LSC Communications
40551612   2020
www.doverpublications.com

Contents

Note

Jack London (1876–1916), born to a childhood of poverty and hardship, lived a life that was as tough and adventure-filled as his stories. An oyster pirate, a government patrolman, a sailor, a social activist, a gold prospector, a university lecturer, to name just a few of his occupations, he was also a self-taught writer who became America's most popular and highly paid author.

He wrote *Call of the Wild* for children in 1903. It is the story of Buck, an intelligent and heroic dog, who is stolen from his comfortable home in sunny California and transported to the frozen North. Beaten into submission, he is forced to adapt to the grueling existence of a sled dog. Written with power and wisdom, as seen through Buck's eyes, *Call of the Wild* follows this powerful beast as he endures great suffering, takes control of his life, and leaves civilization behind. In a time when proper Victorian behavior and sentimentality ruled the day, the brutal *Call of the Wild* was an instant success with readers of all ages. Forging new paths in American literature, it remains one of the most gripping adventure and dog stories ever written.

1. Into the Primitive

BUCK DID not read the newspapers, or he would have known that trouble was brewing, not only for himself, but for every strong, long-haired dog from Seattle to San Diego. The trouble was coming because men, far away in the Arctic, had found gold, and because thousands of men were rushing into the Northland. These men wanted dogs, and the dogs they wanted were large dogs with strong muscles for work and furry coats to protect them from the frost.

Buck lived at a big house in the sun-kissed Santa Clara Valley in California. It was called Judge Miller's place and stood back from the road among the trees. There were stables in back, rows of servants' cottages covered with vines, green pastures, orchards and berry patches. Then there was the pumping plant for the well, and the big cement tank where Judge Miller's men took their morning plunge and kept cool in the hot afternoon.

And Buck ruled over this great estate. Here he was born, and here had lived the four years of his life. There were other dogs, of course, but they did not count to Buck. They came and went, or lived in the house and rarely ventured outside. But Buck was neither house-dog nor common dog. The whole estate was his. He plunged into the swimming tank or went hunting with the Judge's sons; he escorted Mollie and Alice, the Judge's daughters, on long twilight or early morning rambles; on wintry

He lay at the Judge's feet before the library fireplace.

nights he lay at the Judge's feet before the library fireplace; he carried the Judge's grandsons on his back, or rolled them in the grass and guarded their footsteps through wild adventures down to the fountain in the stable yard, and even beyond, where the paddocks were, and the berry patches.

His father, Elmo, a huge Saint Bernard, had been the Judge's inseparable companion, and Buck tried to follow his father in the Judge's affections. He was not so large as Elmo—he weighed only one hundred and forty pounds—because his mother, Shep, had been a Scotch shepherd dog. Nevertheless, those one hundred and forty pounds enabled him to carry himself in a royal fashion. During the four years since his puppyhood, he had lived the life of a prince; he had pride in himself. But he had not let himself become a mere pampered house-dog. Hunting and other outdoor activities had kept down the fat and hardened his muscles.

This was the dog Buck's life in the fall of 1897, when the Klondike gold rush dragged men from all the world into the frozen North. Buck did not know that Manuel, one of the gardener's helpers, read the newspapers. Manuel's vice was that he loved gambling, and so always needed more money than he earned.

The Judge was at a meeting of the Raisin Growers' Association, and the boys were busy on the memorable night of Manuel's crime. No one saw him and Buck go off through the orchard on what Buck imagined was merely a stroll. When they arrived at the little train station a strange man talked with Manuel and passed money to him.

"You might wrap up the goods before you deliver 'em!" the stranger said.

So Manuel wrapped a piece of thick rope around Buck's neck under the collar.

"Twist it, and you'll choke 'im plenty," said Manuel, and the stranger grunted, "All righty."

Buck had accepted the rope; he had learned to trust in men he knew and to give them credit for a wisdom that outreached his own. But when the ends of the rope were placed in the stranger's hands, he growled. To his surprise the rope tightened around his neck, shutting off his breath. In quick rage he sprang at the man, who met him halfway, grappled him by the throat, and with a twist threw Buck over on his back. Then the rope tightened, while Buck struggled in a fury, his tongue sticking out of his mouth and his chest panting. Never in all his life had he been so cruelly treated, and never in all his life had he been so angry. But the next thing he knew, after passing out, was when the train stopped and the two men threw him into the baggage car.

When he awoke again from the choking, he knew where he was, for he had travelled enough with the Judge to know what it was like to ride in a baggage car. He opened his eyes and was furious. The man sprang for his throat, but Buck was too quick for him. His jaws closed on the hand, and they did not relax and open until the man had choked his senses out of him once more.

In San Francisco that night, some men filed the heavy brass collar from his neck, and then Buck was flung into a cagelike crate.

There he lay for the remainder of the weary night, nursing his anger and wounded pride. He could not understand what it all meant. What did they want with him, these strange men? Why were they keeping him boxed up in this crate? He did not know why, but he felt something terrible was sure to come. Several times during the night he sprang to his feet when the shed door rattled open, expecting to see the Judge. But each time it was a fat face that peered in at him by the light of a candle. And each time Buck gave a savage growl at him.

But the man let him alone, and in the morning four men entered and picked up the crate. He stormed and raged at them through the bars. They only laughed and poked sticks at him, which he promptly attacked with his teeth till he realized that was what they wanted. So he lay down unhappily and allowed the crate to be lifted into a wagon. Then he, and the crate in which he was imprisoned, began a passage through many hands. Clerks in the cargo office took charge of him; he was carted about in another wagon; a truck carried him, with an assortment of boxes and parcels, upon a ferry steamer; then he was trucked off the steamer into a railway depot, and finally he was put on a train.

For two days and nights the train rolled on. For two days and nights Buck neither ate nor drank. He tried to attack the men who approached his cage. It was all very silly, he knew; he did not mind the hunger so much, but the lack of water caused him severe suffering and fanned his anger.

He was glad of one thing: the rope was off his neck. That had given them an unfair advantage; but now that it was off, he would show them. They would never get another rope around his neck. He was sure about that. The train workers breathed with relief when they bundled off this raging fiend from the boxcar in Seattle.

Four men carefully carried the crate from the wagon into a small, high-walled backyard. A large, heavy man in a red sweater came out and signed for the crate. That was the man, Buck decided, who would be his next tormentor, and he hurled himself savagely against the bars. The man smiled grimly, and pulled out a hatchet and a club from a bag.

"You ain't going to take him out now?" the driver asked.

"Sure," the man replied, driving the hatchet into the crate.

The four men who had carried it scattered, and from safe perches on top of the wall they waited to watch.

Buck rushed at the splintering wood, sinking his teeth into it, wrestling with it. Wherever the hatchet fell on the outside, there he was on the inside, snarling and growling, as anxious to get out as the man was to get him out.

"Now, you red-eyed devil," the man said, when he had made an opening large enough for Buck's body. He dropped the hatchet and shifted the club to his right hand.

And Buck was truly a red-eyed devil as he drew himself together for the spring, hair bristling, mouth foaming, a mad glitter in his blood-shot eyes. He launched himself straight at the man. In midair, just as his jaws were about to close on the man, he received a shock that checked his body and brought his teeth together with an agonizing snap. He whirled over, falling to the ground on his back and side. He had never been struck by a club in his life, and did not understand. With a snarl that was part bark and more scream he was again on his feet and launched into the air. And again the shock of the club's blow came and he was brought crushingly to the ground. But his madness would not let him stop his attacks on the man. A dozen times he charged, and as often the club broke the charge and smashed him down.

After a particularly fierce blow Buck crawled to his feet,

He launched himself straight at the man.

too dazed to rush. He staggered limply about, the blood flowing from nose and mouth and ears, his beautiful coat sprayed and flecked with blood. Then the man came after him and deliberately dealt him a blow on the nose. All the pain he had endured was nothing compared to this! With a roar he again hurled himself at the man. But the man, shifting the club from right to left, coolly caught him on the lower jaw. Buck crashed to the ground on his head and chest.

For the last time he rushed. The man struck another blow, and Buck crumpled up and went down, knocked utterly senseless.

"He's no slouch at dog-breakin', that's what I say," said one of the men on the wall.

Buck's senses slowly came back to him, but not his strength. He lay where he had fallen, and from there he watched the man in the red sweater.

"'Answers to the name of Buck!'" the red-sweatered man said aloud, reading from the kidnapper's letter. "Well,

Buck, my boy," he went on in a kind voice, "we've had our little battle, and the best thing we can do is to let it go at that. You've learned your place, and I know mine. Be a good dog, and all will go well. Be a bad dog, and I'll whale the stuffin' outa you. Understand?"

As he spoke he fearlessly patted the head he had just been striking, and though Buck's hair bristled at the touch of the hand, he endured it. When the man brought him water he drank, and later he ate a large meal of raw meat offered by the man's open hand.

Buck had been beaten, but he was not broken. He saw that he stood no chance against a man with a club. He had learned the lesson, and he never forgot it.

As days went by, other dogs came in crates and at the ends of ropes, some obediently, some raging and roaring as he had come; and, one and all, he watched them pass under the club of the man in the red sweater.

Now and again men came, strangers, who talked excitedly to the man in the red sweater. And at such times when money passed between them, the strangers took one or more of the dogs away with them. Buck wondered where they went, for they never came back. Then his time came, when a little man who spoke broken English bought him.

"Dat one bully dog!" he said when he first saw Buck. "Eh? How moch?"

"Three hundred," replied the man in the red sweater. "And seein' it's the government payin', you shouldn't have a hard time swallowin' that, eh, Perrault?"

Perrault grinned. Considering that the price of dogs had been booming skyward due to the high demand, it was not an unfair price. The Canadian government would not lose out on this dog, and its mail would travel faster. Perrault knew dogs, and when he looked at Buck he knew that he was one in ten thousand.

Buck saw money pass between them, and was not surprised when Curly, a good-natured Newfoundland, and he were led away by the little man. That was the last he ever

saw of the man in the red sweater, and as he and Curly
looked back at Seattle from the deck of a ship, it was the
last he saw of the warm Southland. In between decks of
the ship, Buck and Curly joined two other dogs. One of
them was a big, snow-white fellow who had accompanied
a Geological Survey across northern Canada. He was a
friendly dog, in a sneaky way, smiling into one's face while
he stole. For instance, he stole from Buck's food at the
first meal. As Buck sprang to punish him, Perrault's partner, a man named Francois, lashed the culprit first; and
nothing remained to Buck but to recover the bone. That
was fair of Francois, Buck decided.

The other dog was a gloomy, sad fellow, and he showed
that all he desired was to be left alone, that there would
be trouble if he were not. He was called Dave, and he took
interest in nothing, not even when the ship rolled and
pitched and hopped in the choppy seas.

Day and night the ship went on with the tireless propeller noisily going, and though one day was very like another, Buck noticed that the weather was steadily growing
colder. At last, one morning, the propeller was quiet, and
the ship was full of excitement. Buck felt it, as did the
other dogs, and knew that a change was coming. Francois
leashed them and brought them on deck. At the first step
upon the cold surface, Buck's feet sank into a white
mushy something; it was very much like mud. He sprang
back with a snort. More of this white stuff was falling
through the air. He shook himself, but more of it fell upon
him. He sniffed it, then licked some up on his tongue. It bit
like fire, and the next instant it was gone. This puzzled
him. He tried it again, with the same result. The men
watching him laughed. It was Buck's first snow.

2. The Law of Club and Fang

BUCK'S FIRST day in his new home was a nightmare. Every hour was filled with shock and surprise. All was confusion and action, and every moment he had to be alert. He discovered that these dogs and men were not civilized. They were savages, all of them, who knew no law but the law of the club and fang. He had never seen dogs fight as these wolfish creatures fought. Curly was the victim of the first fight Buck witnessed. They were camped near the log store, where Curly, in her friendly way, approached a husky dog not half as large as she. There was no warning, only a leap in a flash, a scissoring clip of the teeth, a leap out, and Curly's face was ripped open from eye to jaw.

It was the wolf manner of fighting, to strike and leap away; but there was more to it than this. Thirty or forty huskies ran to the spot and surrounded the combatants in a circle. Curly rushed her attacker, who struck again and leaped aside. He met her next rush with his chest, which tumbled her off her feet. She never got up again. This was what the onlooking huskies had waited for. They closed in upon her, snarling and yelping, and she was buried, screaming with agony, beneath the horde.

Francois, swinging an axe, sprang into the mess of dogs. Three men with clubs were helping him to scatter them. Two minutes from the time Curly fell to the ground, the last of her attackers were clubbed away. But Curly lay

9

there limp and dead in the bloody snow. This scene often came back to Buck and troubled him in his sleep. So that was the way, he realized. No fair play. Once down, that was the end of you. Well, he would see to it that he never went down.

Before he had recovered from the shock caused by the tragic death of Curly, he received another shock. Francois fastened upon him an arrangement of straps and buckles. It was a harness, such as he had seen the men put on the horses at home in California. And as he had seen horses work, so he was set to work, hauling Francois on a sled to the forest that fringed the valley, and returning with a load of firewood. Though he disliked being made a work-dog, he was too wise to rebel. He buckled down with a will and did his best, though it was all new and strange. Francois was stern, demanding instant obedience, and got it by the use of his whip; while Dave, the dog behind Buck, nipped Buck's hind quarters whenever he made a mistake. Spitz was the leader, and he growled sharply at Buck now and again. Buck learned easily, and made remarkable progress. Before they returned to camp he knew enough to stop at "Ho," to go ahead at "Mush," to swing wide on the bends, and to keep clear of the dog behind when the loaded sled shot downhill at their heels.

"Dese tree is ver good dogs!" Francois told Perrault. "Dat Buck, heem pool lak crazy. I tich heem queek as anyting."

By afternoon, Perrault, who was in a hurry to be on the trail with his mail, returned with two huskies, Billee and Joe, two brothers. Sons of one mother though they were, they were as different as day and night. Billee's one fault was he was much too good-natured, while Joe was the very opposite, sour and a loner, with a snarl always on his lip and an evil glimmer always in his eyes. Buck welcomed them in a friendly way, but Dave ignored them, and Spitz proceeded to try to bully first one of them and then the other. Joe would have none of that, and clipped his jaws together at the dog-team leader, but soft Billee, offering no resistance, was driven to the ends of the camp.

By evening Perrault had bought another dog, an old husky, long and lean, with a battle-scarred face and a single eye. He was called Sol-leks, which means the Angry One in the native tribe's language. He did not like to be approached on his blind side, and Buck was unlucky enough to discover this in a painful way. Sol-leks suddenly whirled on him and slashed with his long teeth Buck's shoulder to the bone. Forever after Buck avoided his blind side, and they never had any more trouble. Like Dave, Sol-leks' only desire seemed to be to be left alone.

That night Buck faced the great problem of sleeping. The tent, lit by a candle, glowed warmly in the midst of the snow; and when he decided to enter it, both Perrault and Francois cursed him and threw pots and lids at him till he fled into the outer cold. A chilly wind was blowing that nipped him sharply and bit with special pain into his wounded shoulder. He lay down on the snow and tried to sleep, but the frost soon drove him shivering to his feet. Miserable, he wandered about among the many tents, only to find that one place was as cold as another. Here and there savage dogs rushed upon him, but he bristled his neck-hair and snarled (for he was learning fast), and they let him go on his way.

Finally an idea came to him. He would return and see how his own teammates were making out. To his surprise, they had disappeared. Again he wandered about through the large camp, looking for them, and again he returned. Were they in the tent? No, they could not be, or else he would not have been driven out. Then where could they possibly be? With drooping tail and shivering body, he circled the tent. Suddenly the snow gave way beneath his forelegs and he sank down. Something wriggled under his feet. He sprang back, bristling and snarling. But a friendly little yelp reassured him, and he went back to look. A whiff of warm air came to his nose, and there, curled up under the snow in a snug ball, lay Billee. He whined invitingly, squirmed and wriggled to show his good will.

So that was the way they did it, eh? Buck selected a spot, and proceeded to dig a hole for himself. In a minute the heat from his body filled the tight space and he was asleep. The day had been long and hard, and he slept well, though he growled and barked and wrestled with bad dreams.

He did not open his eyes till roused by the noises of the waking camp. At first he did not know where he was. It had snowed during the night and he was completely buried. The snow walls pressed him on every side, and fear swept through him—that he had been trapped. The muscles of his whole body tightened, the hair on his neck and shoulders stood on end, and with a ferocious snarl he bounded straight up into the blinding day, the snow flying about him in a flashing cloud. Before he landed on his feet, he saw the white camp spread out before him and knew where he was and remembered all that had passed from the time he went for a stroll with Manuel to the hole he had dug for himself the night before.

A shout from Francois greeted him. "Wot I say?" the driver called to Perrault. "Dat Buck for sure learn queek as anyting!"

Perrault nodded. As a man carrying important business for the Canadian government, he was anxious to have the best dogs.

Three more huskies were added to the team that hour, making a total of nine, and before another quarter of an hour had passed they were in harness and swinging up the trail toward the Dyea Canyon. Buck was glad to be away, and though the work was hard he found he did not dislike it.

Dave was wheeler, or sled dog, and pulling in front of him was Buck, then Sol-leks; the rest of the team was strung out ahead, single file, to the leader, Spitz. Buck had been purposefully placed between Dave and Sol-leks so that he might receive instruction. As quick a student as he

Buck had been purposefully placed between Dave and Sol-leks
so that he might receive instruction.

was, they were quick teachers, never allowing him to remain in error for long. Dave was fair, and never nipped Buck without cause. Once, during a brief stop, when he got tangled in the traces and delayed the start, both Dave and Sol-leks flew at him. After that, Buck took good care to keep the traces clear, and before the day was done, he had mastered his work so well that his mates had ceased nagging him.

It was a hard day's run, up the canyon, through Sheep Camp, past the Scales and the timber line, across glaciers and snowdrifts hundreds of feet deep, and over the great Chilkoot Divide, which stands between the salt water and the fresh and guards the sad and lonely North. They made good time down the chain of lakes which fills the craters of extinct volcanoes, and late that night pulled into the huge camp at the head of Lake Bennett, where thousands of gold-seekers were building boats for the time in the spring when the ice would break up. Buck made his hole in the snow and slept deeply, but was woken up early in the cold darkness and harnessed with his mates to the sled.

That day they made forty miles, the trail being packed; but the next day, and for many days to follow, they broke their own trail, worked harder, and made worse time. As a rule, Perrault travelled ahead of the team, packing the snow with webbed shoes to make it easier for them. Francois, guiding the sled, sometimes exchanged places with him, but not often. Perrault was in a hurry, and he prided himself on his knowledge of ice, for the fall ice was very thin, and where there was swift water, there was no ice at all.

Day after day, Buck toiled in the traces. Always, they broke camp in the dark, and the first gray of dawn found them hitting the trail with fresh miles reeled off behind them. And always they pitched camp after dark, eating their bit of fish, and crawling to sleep into the snow. Buck was terribly hungry. The pound and a half of sun-dried salmon, which was his ration for each day, seemed not nearly enough. He suffered from hunger pangs. Yet the other dogs, because they weighed less and were born to the life, received a pound only of the fish and managed to keep in good condition.

He swiftly lost his old eating habits, where he took his time over his meals. For he found here that his mates, finishing first, robbed him of his unfinished ration. There was no defending it. While he was fighting off two or three dogs, it was disappearing down the throats of the others. So he learned to eat as fast as they; and because of his own hunger, he sometimes even stole from them. He watched and learned. When he saw Pike, one of the new dogs, slyly steal a slice of bacon when Perrault's back was turned, he tried the same trick the next day, getting away with a whole chunk.

This first theft marked Buck as fit to survive in the unfriendly world of the North. It marked his ability to adapt to changing conditions. It marked, as well, the going to pieces of his moral nature. It was all well enough in the Southland, under the law of love and fellowship, to respect private property and personal feelings, but in the Northland, under the law of club and fang, it was foolish to do so.

It was not that Buck reasoned this out. He unconsciously adapted himself to the new mode of life. All his days, no matter what the odds, he had never run from a fight. But the club of the man in the red sweater had beaten into him a primitive code. Now, he must always save his own hide. He did not steal for the joy of it, but because of the demands of his stomach. He did not rob openly, but stole secretly and cunningly, out of respect for club and fang.

His physical development was rapid. His muscles became hard as iron and he grew indifferent to all ordinary pain. He could eat anything, and his body was able to use it. His sight and sense of smell became remarkably keen, while his hearing developed such sharpness that in his sleep he heard the faintest sound and knew whether it meant peace or danger. He learned to bite the ice out with his teeth when it collected between his toes; and when he was thirsty and there was a thick coat of ice over the water hole, he would break it by rearing and striking it with stiff forelegs.

And not only did he learn by experience, but instincts long dead became alive again. The domesticated generations fell from him. In vague ways he remembered back to the youth of his breed, to the time when the wild dogs ranged in packs through the ancient forests and killed their meat as they ran it down. It was no task for him to learn to fight with cut and slash and the quick wolf snap. In this manner his ancestors had fought. An old life was renewed in him. When, on the cold, clear nights he pointed his nose at a star and howled long and wolflike, it was his ancestors, dead and dust, pointing nose at star and howling down through centuries and through him.

And the reason he came into a sense of his own deeper self was because men had found a yellow metal in the North; and because Manuel was a gardener's helper whose wages were not enough to pay for the needs of a wife, children and gambling.

3. The Fight for Leadership

BUCK'S NEWBORN cunning gave him poise and control. He was too busy adjusting himself to the new life to feel at ease, and not only did he not pick fights, but he avoided them whenever possible. Even in the bitter hatred between him and Spitz, he showed no impatience, and tried not to offend the pack-leader.

Spitz, however, possibly because he saw in Buck a dangerous rival, never lost a chance of showing his teeth. He even went out of his way to bully Buck, trying constantly to start the fight which could end only in the death of one or the other.

Early in the trip this might have taken place had it not been for an accident. At the end of this day they made camp on the shore of Lake Le Barge. Driving snow, a wind that cut like a white-hot knife and darkness had forced them to grope for a place to stop. They could hardly have picked a worse spot, however. At their backs rose a wall of rock, and Perrault and Francois had to make their fire and spread their blankets on the ice of the lake itself. They had left the tent at Dyea in order to travel light. A few sticks of driftwood furnished them with a fire that thawed through the ice and left them to eat supper in the dark.

Close in under the shelter of the rock, Buck made his nest. It was so snug and warm that he hated to leave it when Francois distributed the fish which he had first thawed over the fire. But when Buck finished his ration and returned, he found his nest occupied by snarling Spitz. Till now Buck had avoided trouble with his enemy, but this was too much. The beast in him roared. He sprang upon Spitz with a fury which surprised them both.

Francois was surprised, too, when he saw the cause of the trouble. "Oh, oh!" he cried to Buck. "Gif it to heem, by Gar! Gif it to heem, the dirty teef!"

Spitz was crying with rage and eagerness as he circled back and forth for a chance to spring in. Buck was no less eager for the fight, but he was cautious as he likewise circled back and forth for the advantage. But it was then that the unexpected happened, the thing that pushed their struggle for leadership far into the future.

A curse from Perrault, the resounding impact of a wooden club upon a bony body, and a shrill yelp of pain revealed chaos in the camp. The men and dogs were suddenly surrounded by a starving band of huskies, eighty or ninety of them, who had scented their camp from a nearby Indian village. They had crept up while Buck and Spitz were fighting, and when the two men attacked these intruders with heavy clubs, they showed their teeth and fought back. They were crazed by the smell of food. Perrault found one with its head buried in the grub-box. His club landed heavily on the ribs, and the grub-box was turned over on the ground. In that instant a couple of dozen of the starving brutes were scrambling for bread and bacon. The clubs fell upon them, but they didn't leave. They yelped and howled, but kept on till the last crumb had been devoured.

In the meantime the astonished team-dogs had burst out of their nests only to be set upon by the invaders. Never had Buck seen such dogs. It seemed as though their bones would burst through their skins. They were mere skeletons, draped loosely in hides, with blazing eyes and slobbering fangs. But their hunger-madness made them terrifying. There was no opposing them. The team-dogs were swept back against the cliff. Buck was attacked by

Buck was attacked by three huskies.

three huskies, and in a moment his head and shoulders were slashed. The din of the barking dogs was frightful. Billee was crying as usual. Dave and Sol-leks, dripping blood from a dozen wounds, were fighting bravely side by side. Joe was snapping like a demon. Once, his teeth closed on the foreleg of a husky, and he crunched the bone. Pike leaped upon the crippled animal, breaking its neck. Buck got another enemy by the throat, and then another—and then felt teeth sink into his own throat. It was Spitz attacking him from the side!

Perrault and Francois, having cleared out their part of the camp, hurried to save their sled-dogs. Buck shook himself free from Spitz, and Francois rushed in and kept the opponents apart.

What an evening this had been! The huskies had torn away half of the food supplies before they were run off by the men. The huskies had chewed through the sled lashings and canvas coverings. Nothing, no matter how remotely eatable, had escaped them. They had eaten a pair

of Perrault's moose-hide moccasins and even two feet of
lash from the end of Francois' whip. The nine sled-dogs,
meanwhile, were in a sorry state. There was not one who
was not wounded in four or five places. Dub was badly in-
jured in a hind leg; Dolly, the last husky added to the team
at Dyea, had a badly torn throat; Joe had lost an eye; while
Billee, with an ear chewed and cut to ribbons, cried and
whimpered through the night.

"Ah, my frens!" Francois said, "mebbe it mek you mad
dogs, dose many bites. Mebbe all mad dog! Wot you think,
eh, Perrault?"

The mail-runner shook his head. With four hundred
miles of trail still between them and Dawson, he could ill
afford to have madness break out among his dogs. Two
hours of work got the harnesses into shape, and the
wounded team was under way, struggling painfully over
the hardest part of the trail.

The Thirty Mile River was running wide open. Its wild
water defied the freeze, and it was in the eddies only and
in the quiet places that the ice held at all. Six days of hard
work were required for those thirty terrible miles. Every
foot put them at risk of life. A dozen times, Perrault, nos-
ing the way, broke through the ice bridges, being saved by
a long pole he carried, holding it so that it fell each time
across the hole made by his body. But a cold snap was on,
the thermometer registering fifty below zero, and each
time he broke through he was compelled to build a fire
and dry his garments.

Once, the sled broke through, with Dave and Buck
falling into the water, and they were half-frozen and all but
drowned by the time they were dragged out. The usual
fire was necessary to save them. They were coated solidly
with ice, and the two men kept them on the run around
the fire, sweating and thawing.

At another time Spitz went through, dragging the whole
team after him up to Buck, who strained backward with all
his might, his forepaws on the slippery edge and the ice
quivering and snapping all around. But behind him was

Dave, likewise straining backward, and behind the sled was Francois, pulling.

Again, the rim ice broke away ahead and behind, and there was no escape except up a cliff. Night found them back on the river with a quarter of a mile to the day's credit.

By the time they made the Houtalinqua River and good ice, Buck was exhausted. The rest of the dogs were the same, but Perrault, to make up lost time, pushed them late and early. The first day they covered thirty-five miles to the Big Salmon River; the next day thirty-five more to the Little Salmon; the third day forty miles, which brought them well up toward the Five Fingers.

Buck's feet were not so compact and hard as the feet of the huskies. His had softened during the many generations since the day his last wild ancestor was tamed by a cave-dweller. All day long he limped in agony, and, once camp was made, lay down like a dead dog. Hungry as he was, he would not move to receive his ration of fish, which Francois had to bring to him. Also, the dog-driver rubbed Buck's feet for half an hour each night after supper, and cut off the tops of his own moccasins to make four moccasins for Buck. This was a great relief, and Buck caused even the stiff face of Perrault to twist itself into a grin one morning, when Francois forgot the moccasins and Buck lay on his back, his four feet waving in the air, and refused to budge without them. Later his feet grew hard to the trail, and the worn-out footgear was thrown away.

Spitz, as lead dog and master of the team, felt threatened by this strange Southland dog. Buck matched the husky in strength, savagery and cunning. It was no surprise that the clash for leadership should come. Buck wanted it. To provoke Spitz's anger, he would come between the pack-leader and the wayward dogs who should have been punished. One night there was a heavy snowfall, and in the morning Pike did not appear. He was hidden in his nest under a foot of snow. Francois called him and looked for him. Spitz was wild with wrath for the delay. He raged through the camp, smelling and digging in every likely place, snarling so frightfully that Pike heard and shivered in his hiding-place.

But when he was at last uncovered, and Spitz flew at him to punish him, Buck flew in between. So unexpected was it that Spitz was thrown backward and off his feet. Buck and Pike sprang upon the overthrown leader. But Francois brought his lash down upon Buck, until Buck was knocked away, while Spitz soundly punished Pike.

In the days that followed, as Dawson drew closer, Buck still continued to interfere between Spitz and the culprits; but he did it only when Francois was not around. With this secret mutiny of Buck, a general chaos sprang up. Dave and Sol-leks stayed true to their tasks, but the rest of the team went from bad to worse. Things no longer went right. There was continual bickering.

But finally they pulled into Dawson one dreary afternoon. Here were many men, and countless dogs, and Buck found them all at work. All day they ran up and down the main street, and in the night their jingling bells still went by. In this town dogs hauled cabin logs and firewood, and did all manner of work that horses did in California. Occasionally Buck met Southland dogs, but for the most part they were the wild wolf-husky breed. Every night they howled a weird and eerie chant, which Buck was delighted to join in.

Seven days from the time they pulled into Dawson, they dropped down the steep bank by the Barracks to the Yukon Trail, and pulled for Dyea and Salt Water. Perrault was carrying important mail, and he wanted them to make the trip in record time. The week's rest had allowed the dogs to heal and put them in good shape. The trail they had broken was packed hard by later journeyers. Not only that, there were two or three places where officials had left grub for dogs and men.

They made Sixty Miles, which is a fifty-mile run, on the

first day; and the second day saw them booming up the Yukon well on their way to Pelly. But the revolt led by Buck had destroyed the cooperation of the team. No more was Spitz a leader to be greatly feared. The dogs began challenging his authority. Pike robbed him of half a fish one night, and gulped it down under the protection of Buck. Another night Dub and Joe fought Spitz and made him give up on punishing them as they deserved. And even Billee, the good-natured one, was less good-natured. Buck never came near Spitz without snarling and bristling.

The breaking down of discipline likewise affected the dogs in their relations with one another. They fought and bickered more than ever among themselves, till at times the camp was howling. Francois cursed them, stamped the snow, and tore his hair. His lash was always singing among the dogs, but it was of little help. As soon as he turned his back they were at it again. He backed up Spitz with his whip, while Buck backed up the remainder of the team. Francois knew Buck was behind all the trouble, but Buck was too clever to be caught red-handed.

At the mouth of the Tahkeena, one night after supper, Dub frightened a snowshoe rabbit and tore off after it. In a second the whole team was in full cry. A hundred yards away was the camp of the Northwest Police, with fifty huskies, who joined the chase. The rabbit sped down the river, turned off into a small creek, along its frozen bed. It ran lightly on the surface of the snow, while the dogs plowed through it. Buck led the pack, sixty strong, around bend after bend, sounding the old wolf-cry, straining after the food that fled swiftly before him through the moonlight.

But Spitz left the pack and cut across a narrow neck of land where the creek made a long bend around. Buck did not know of this, and as he rounded the bend, the snowy rabbit still flitting before him, he saw the figure of Spitz leap from the overhanging bank into the path of the rabbit. The rabbit could not turn, and Spitz's white teeth broke its back in midair. The full pack at Buck's heels raised a yelping chorus of delight.

But Buck did not cry out. He drove in upon Spitz, knocking him over into the powdery snow. In an instant, however, Spitz gained his feet and slashed Buck down the shoulder and leaped clear. Twice Spitz's teeth clipped together, like the steel jaws of a trap, as he backed away for better footing, snarling.

Buck knew the time had come. It was to the death. They circled about, snarling, ears laid back, watchful for an opening. The other dogs, meanwhile, drew up around them in a circle. Their eyes were gleaming.

Spitz was a practiced fighter. Through the Arctic and across Canada, he had held his own against all manner of

They circled about, snarling, ears laid back, watchful for an opening.

dogs. He never rushed till he was prepared to receive a rush; never attacked till he had first defended that attack.

Try as he would Buck could not sink his teeth in the neck of the big white dog. Wherever his fangs struck for the softer flesh, they were countered by the fangs of Spitz. Fang against fang, their lips were cut and bleeding. Then Buck warmed up and made a series of rushes at Spitz. Time and time again he tried for the snow-white throat, but each and every time Spitz slashed him and got away. Then Buck took to rushing, as though for the throat, when, suddenly drawing back his head and curving in from the side, he would drive his shoulder at the shoulder of Spitz, to try to knock him over. But instead, Buck's shoulder was slashed each time as Spitz leaped lightly away.

Spitz was untouched, while Buck was streaming with blood and panting hard. The fight was desperate. All the while the silent and wolfish circle waited to finish off whichever dog went down. As Buck became tired, Spitz took to rushing, and he kept him staggering. Once Buck went over and the whole circle of sixty dogs started up; but he recovered, almost in midair, and the circle sank down again and waited.

Fortunately Buck had imagination. He fought by instinct, but he could fight by brains as well. He rushed, as though attempting the old shoulder trick, but at the last instant swept low to the snow and in. His teeth closed on Spitz's left foreleg. There was a crunch of breaking bone, and the white dog faced him on three legs. Three times he tried to knock him over, then repeated the trick and broke the right foreleg. Spitz struggled to keep up. He saw the silent circle, with gleaming eyes, lolling tongues, and silvery breaths drifting upward, closing in upon him as he had seen similar circles close in upon beaten enemies in the past. Only this time he was the one who was beaten.

There was no hope for him. Buck got ready for the final rush. The circle had tightened till he could feel the breaths of the huskies on his flanks. He could see them,

beyond Spitz and to either side, half-crouching for the
spring, their eyes fixed upon him. Spitz staggered back
and forth, snarling with menace. Then Buck sprang in and
out, but while he was in, his shoulder squarely met
Spitz's, and the one-time pack-leader tumbled to the
ground. The dark circle became a dot on the moon-
flooded snow as Spitz disappeared from view. Buck stood
and looked on, the successful champion, the dominant
beast who had made his kill.

4. Mastership

THE NEXT MORNING Francois discovered Spitz missing and Buck covered with wounds.

"Dat Spitz fight lak crazy," said Perrault.

"An' dat Buck fight lak two crazies," was Francois' answer. "An' now we make good time. No more Spitz, no more trouble, for sure."

While Perrault packed the camp outfit and loaded the sled, the dog-driver harnessed the dogs. Buck trotted up to the place Spitz would have occupied as leader; but Francois, not noticing him, brought Sol-leks to the lead position. In Francois' judgment, Sol-leks was the best lead-dog left, but Buck sprang upon Sol-leks in a fury.

"Ha, ha!" cried Francois. "Look at dat Buck. Him kill dat Spitz, him tink to take de job!—Now, go 'way, Buck!"

But Buck refused to budge.

Francois took Buck by the scruff of the neck, dragged him to one side and replaced Sol-leks. The old dog did not like it, and showed that he was afraid of Buck. When Francois turned his back, Buck again displaced Sol-leks.

Buck wanted to have the leadership. It was his! He had earned it, and he would not be content with less.

Francois sat down and scratched his head. Perrault looked at his watch and swore. Time was flying, and they should have been on the trail an hour before. Francois shook his head and grinned at his partner, who shrugged his shoulders to say that they were beaten. Then Francois went up and fastened the traces to Buck. A few moments

27

later, the sled broke out, and with both men running they dashed out on to the river trail.

From the first step, Buck took up the duties of leadership; and where judgment was required, and quick thinking and quick acting, he showed himself superior even to Spitz, of whom Francois had never seen an equal.

But it was in giving the law and making his mates live up to it that Buck excelled. Dave and Sol-leks did not mind the change in leadership. Most of the team, however, had grown unruly during the last days of Spitz, and their surprise was great now that Buck worked them into shape.

Pike, who pulled at Buck's heels, and who never pulled more than he had to, was swiftly and repeatedly shaken for loafing, and before the first day was done he was pulling more than ever before in his life. The first night in camp, Joe, a sour dog, was punished soundly—a thing that Spitz had never managed to do.

The general tone of the team picked up immediately. It recovered its old-time teamwork, and once more the dogs leaped as one dog in the traces. At the Rink Rapids two native huskies, Teek and Koona, were added, and the quickness with which Buck broke them in took away Francois' breath.

"Nevaire such a dog as dat Buck!" he cried. "Him worth one t'ousand dollar, eh? Wot you say, Perrault?"

And Perrault nodded. The trail was in excellent condition, well-packed and hard, and there was no new-fallen snow with which to contend. It was not too cold. The temperature dropped to fifty below zero and remained there the whole trip. The men rode and ran by turn, and the dogs were kept on the go.

The Thirty Mile River was comparatively coated with ice, and they covered in one day going out what had taken ten days coming in. In one run they made a sixty-mile dash. Across Marsh, Tagish, and Bennett (seventy miles of lakes), they flew so fast that the man whose turn it was to run towed behind the sled at the end of a rope. And on the last night of the second week they topped White Pass and dropped down the sea slope with the lights of Skagway at their feet.

It was a record run. Each day for fourteen days they had averaged forty miles. For three days Perrault and Francois were kings of Skagway, and the dogs were admired. But within that week, Francois and Perrault received new official orders and had to go say goodbye to their dogs. Francois threw his arms around Buck and wept over him. Like other men, these two passed out of Buck's life for good.

Another man took charge of him and his mates, and in company with a dozen other dog-teams he started back over the weary trail to Dawson. It was no light running now, nor record time, but heavy toil each day, with a heavy load behind; for this was the mail train, carrying word from the world to the men who looked for gold in the Far North.

Buck did not like it, but he bore up well to the work, and saw that his mates did their fair share. It was a dull life, one day very much like another. At a certain time each morning the cooks woke, built fires, and the men and dogs ate. Then while some packed up the camp, others harnessed the dogs, and they were under way an hour or so before dawn. At night, camp was made. Some pitched the tents, others cut firewood and pine bows for the beds, and still others carried water or ice for the cooks. Also, the dogs were fed.

Afterwards, Buck loved to lie near the fire, hind legs crouched under him, forelegs stretched out in front, head raised, and eyes blinking dreamily at the flames. Sometimes he thought of Judge Miller's big house in the sun-kissed Santa Clara Valley; but more often he remembered the man in the red sweater, the death of Curly, the great fight with Spitz and the good things he had eaten or would like to eat. He was not homesick. He began to have memories of a past he had never seen. The instincts of a wild dog were coming back to him.

It was a hard trip, with the mail behind them, and the

heavy work wore them down. They were in poor condition when they made Dawson, and should have had a ten days' or a week's rest at least. But in two days' time they dropped down the Yukon, loaded with letters for the outside. The dogs were tired, the drivers grumbling, and to make matters worse it snowed every day. This meant soft trail and heavier pulling for the dogs; yet the drivers were fair through it all, and did their best for the animals.

Each night the dogs were attended to first. They ate before the drivers ate, and no man got into his sleeping-bag till he had seen to the feet of the dogs he drove. Still, their strength went down. Since the beginning of the winter they had travelled eighteen hundred miles, dragging sleds the whole weary distance. Buck stood up to the work, keeping his mates up to their work and maintaining discipline, though he too was very tired.

Thirty days from the time they left Dawson, Buck and his mates arrived at Skagway. They were in a wretched state, worn out. Buck's one hundred and forty pounds had dropped to one hundred and fifteen. The rest of his mates had lost much weight. They were all terribly footsore. No spring was left in them. Their feet fell heavily on the trail, jarring their bodies. There was nothing the matter with them except they were dead tired. It was not the dead-tiredness that comes through brief and excessive effort, from which recovery is a matter of hours; but it was the dead-tiredness that comes through the slow and prolonged toil of months. Every muscle, every fiber, every cell, was tired, dead tired. And there was reason for it.

"Mush on, poor sore-feets," the driver called to them as they tottered down the main street of Skagway. "Dis is de last. Den we get one long res'. One bully long res'."

The drivers expected a long stopover. Themselves, they had covered a great distance with two days' rest, and they deserved a stretch of loafing. But so many were the men who had rushed into the Klondike, and so many were the sweethearts, wives, and kin that had not rushed in, that the amount of mail was huge. Also there was official, governmental mail. Fresh batches of dogs were to take the places of those worthless for the trail. The worn-out ones, including Buck and his team, were to be sold.

Three days passed, by which time Buck and his mates found how really tired and weak they were. Then, on the morning of the fourth day, two men from the United States came along and bought them, harness and all, for next to nothing. The men addressed each other as "Hal" and "Charles." Charles was a middle-aged, light-haired man with a moustache. Hal was a youngster of nineteen or twenty, with a big revolver and a hunting-knife strapped about him on a cartridge-heavy belt. Both men seemed out of place in the wild north.

Buck saw the money pass between the man and the government agent, and knew that the mail-train drivers were leaving his life. When brought with his mates to the new owners' camp, Buck saw a sloppily erected tent, unwashed dishes, everything in disorder; also, he saw a woman, "Mercedes," the men called her. She was Charles' wife and Hal's sister.

Buck watched them as they proceeded to take down the tent and load the sled in an awkward manner.

Three men from a neighboring tent came out and looked on, grinning and winking at one another.

"You've got a right neat load!" said one of them. "Think it'll ride? It seems a mite top-heavy."

Charles turned his back on his critics and drew the lashings down as well as he could, which was not well.

"An' of course the dogs can hike along all day with that pile behind them," said another of the men.

"Certainly they will," said Hal, taking hold of the gee-pole with one hand and swinging his whip from the other. "Mush!" he shouted. "Mush on there!"

The dogs sprang against their breastbands, strained hard for a few moments, then relaxed. They were unable to move the sled.

"The lazy brutes, I'll show them," said Hal, preparing to lash them with the whip.

But Mercedes cried out, "No, Hal, you mustn't! The poor dears!"

"They're lazy, I tell you," said her brother, "and you've got to whip them to get anything out of them. You ask anyone. Ask any of those men."

"They're weak as water, if you want to know," came the reply from one of the men. "Plumb tuckered out, that's what's the matter. They need a rest."

Now Mercedes changed her tune, not liking the onlookers, and feeling loyal to her brother. "Never mind that man, Hal. You're driving our dogs and you do what you think best with them."

Hal's whip fell upon the dogs. They threw themselves against the breastbands, dug their feet into the packed snow, got down low to it and put forth all their strength. The sled held as though it were an anchor. After two efforts, they stood still, panting. But once more Mercedes interfered. She dropped on her knees before Buck, with tears in her eyes, and put her arms around his neck.

"You poor, poor dear," she cried. "Why don't you pull hard? Then you wouldn't be whipped."

One of the onlookers spoke up: "It's not that I care a whoop what becomes of you folks, but for the dogs' sakes I just want to tell you, you can help them a mighty lot by breaking out that sled. The runners are frozen stuck. Throw your weight against the gee-pole, right and left, and break it out."

Following the advice, this time Hal broke out the runners. The overloaded sled forged ahead, Buck and his mates struggling under the rain of blows from Hal. A hundred yards ahead the path turned and sloped steeply into the main street. It would have required an experienced man to keep the top-heavy sled upright, and Hal was not such a man. As they swung on the turn the sled tipped over, spilling half its load through the loose lashings. The dogs never stopped. The lightened sled bounded on its side behind them. They were angry because of the ill treatment they had received and the far too heavy load.

Buck was raging. He broke into a run, the team following his lead. Hal cried, "Whoa! whoa!" but they did not listen. Hal tripped and was pulled off his feet. The capsized sled ran over him, and the dogs dashed on up to the street.

Kind-hearted citizens caught the dogs and gathered up the scattered belongings. Also, they gave advice. Half the load and twice the dogs, if they ever expected to reach Dawson. Hal and his sister and brother-in-law listened, pitched tent and overhauled their load.

The outfit, though cut in half, was still huge. Charles and Hal went out in the evening and bought six dogs. These, added to the six of the original team, and Teek and Koona, brought the number of dogs to fourteen. But the new dogs did not amount to much. Three were short-haired pointers, one was a Newfoundland, and the other two were mongrels. These newcomers did not seem to know anything. Buck and his comrades looked upon them with disgust, and though he quickly taught them their places and what not to do, he could not teach what to do. They did not like the harnesses or the trail.

With the newcomers hopeless, and the old team worn out by twenty-five hundred miles, the outlook was not bright. The two men, however, were quite cheerful. And they were proud, too. They were doing the thing in style, with fourteen dogs. In the nature of Arctic travel there was a reason why fourteen dogs should not drag one sled, and that was that one sled could not carry the food for fourteen dogs. But Charles and Hal did not know this. They had worked the trip out with a pencil, so much to a dog, so many dogs, and so many days. It was all so very simple.

Late next morning Buck led the long team up the street. There was nothing lively about it, no snap or go in him and his fellows. They were starting dead weary. Buck's heart was not in the work, nor was the heart of any dog. Buck felt that there was no depending upon these two men and the woman. They did not know how to do anything, and as the days went by it became clear that they could not learn. They were slack in all things, without order. It took them half the night to pitch a sloppy camp, and half the morning to break that camp and get the sled loaded. Some days they did not make ten miles. On other days they were unable to get started at all.

It was not long before they went short on dog-food. The men overfed them at first, because they did not understand it was not food the dogs needed, but rest. They were making poor time, and the heavy load they dragged sapped the dogs' strength.

Then came the underfeeding. Hal awoke one day to the fact that his dog-food was half gone and the distance only a quarter covered, and there was no way to buy more food. So he cut down the standard ration and tried to increase the day's travel. It was a simple matter to give the dogs less food; but it was impossible to make the dogs travel faster.

The new dogs began to die off, only the mongrels hanging on to life for some time before being starved and worked to death. Mercedes no longer cared about the remaining dogs, and because she was sore and tired, she rode in the sled. She weighed one hundred and twenty pounds—a cruel extra weight for weak and starving animals. She rode for days, till the dogs fell in their traces and the sled stood still. Charles and Hal begged her to get off and walk, pleaded with her, while she wept and told them they were brutal.

At the Five Fingers the dog-food gave out, and an old Indian woman offered to trade them a few pounds of frozen horsehide for the Colt revolver that Hal was so proud of. Hal made the trade, but the rawhide was almost inedible for even the iron-stomached dogs.

Buck staggered along at the head of the team as in a nightmare. He pulled when he could; when he could no longer pull, he fell down and remained down till blows from whip or club drove him to his feet again. All the gloss had gone from his beautiful furry coat. His muscles had wasted away, so that each rib and every bone in his frame were outlined cleanly through the loose hide. As it was with Buck, so it was with his mates. They were walking skeletons. They were seven all together, including him. When a halt was made, they dropped down in the traces like dead dogs.

There came a day when Billee, the good-natured dog, fell and could not rise. He died, and the next day Koona went. Buck was almost blind with weakness, and he kept the trail by the dim feel of his feet.

It was beautiful spring weather, but neither dogs nor humans were aware of it. Each day the sun rose earlier and set later. It was dawn by three in the morning, and twilight lingered till nine at night. The whole long day was a blaze of sunshine. The ghostly winter silence had given way to the great spring murmur of awakening life. The sap was rising in the pines. The willows and aspens were bursting out in young buds. Crickets sang in the nights, and in the days all manner of creeping, crawling things rustled forth into the sun. Partridges and woodpeckers were booming and knocking in the forest. Squirrels were chattering, birds singing.

From every hill slope came the trickle of running water. All things were thawing, bending, snapping. Thin sections of ice fell through into the river. And amid all this bursting awakening of life, under the blazing sun and the soft-sighing breezes, the two men, the woman and the huskies staggered toward death.

With the dogs falling, Mercedes weeping and riding, Hal swearing and Charles feeling hopeless, they reached a lone man's camp at the mouth of the White River. When they halted, the dogs dropped down as though they had all been struck dead. Hal approached the gold-miner named John Thornton, who was whittling the last touches on an axe-handle. Thornton said, "Don't go any further up the trail. The ice is rotten."

Hal said, "They told us up above that the bottom was

dropping out of the trail and that the best thing for us to do was to lay over. They told us we couldn't make White River, and here we are."

"And they told you the truth," Thornton answered. "The bottom's likely to drop out at any moment. Only fools could have made it. I tell you straight: I wouldn't risk my carcass on that ice for all the gold in Alaska."

"That's because you're not a fool, I suppose," said Hal. "All the same, we'll go to Dawson." He uncoiled his whip. "Get up there, Buck! Hya! Get up there! Mush!"

But neither Buck nor his team got up. The whip continued to flash out, and Thornton sat up and glared at the young man. Sol-leks was the first dog to crawl to his feet. Teek followed. Joe came next, yelping with pain. Pike made painful efforts, and on the third attempt managed to rise. Buck made no effort. He lay quietly where he had fallen. The lash of the whip bit into him again and again, but he neither whined nor struggled. Several times Thornton started to speak out in anger at the foolish man, but he held his tongue.

Hal picked up his club. Buck even now refused to move under the rain of heavy blows. So greatly had he suffered on this trail, and so far gone was he, that the blows did not hurt much. He was almost dead. He felt strangely numb. He could hear the impact of the club upon his hide, but it no longer felt as if it was his body.

And then, suddenly, without warning, with a mad cry, Thornton sprang upon the beast who was clubbing Buck. Hal was hurled backward, and Mercedes screamed.

Thornton protectively stood over Buck, struggling to control himself.

"If you strike that dog again, I'll kill you!" he said.

"It's my dog!" Hal replied. "Get out of my way, or I'll fix you. I'm going to Dawson."

Thornton stood between him and Buck and showed no intention of getting out of the way. The moment Hal drew his long hunting-knife to threaten his foe, Thornton rapped Hal's knuckles with the axe-handle, knocking the

Thornton protectively stood over Buck, struggling to control himself.

knife to the ground. Then Thornton picked up the knife himself and cut Buck's traces.

Hal decided against fighting. A few minutes later he and his wife and brother-in-law pulled out from the bank and down towards the river. Buck heard them go and raised his head to look. Pike was leading, then Sol-leks and Joe and Teek. They were limping and staggering. Mercedes was riding the loaded sled. Hal guided at the gee-pole, and Charles stumbled along in the rear.

As Buck watched them, Thornton knelt beside him and with rough, kindly hands searched for broken bones. By the time his search had shown nothing more than many bruises and a terrible state of starvation, the sled was a quarter of a mile away. Dog and man watched it crawling over the ice. Suddenly, they saw its back end drop down. Mercedes' scream came to their ears. They saw Charles turn and make one step to run back, and then a whole section of ice give way and the dogs and humans disappear. A yawning hole was all that was to be seen. The bottom had dropped out of the trail.

Thornton and Buck looked at each other.

"You poor devil," said Thornton, and Buck licked his hand.

5. For the Love of Man

WHEN JOHN THORNTON froze his feet the previous December, his partners had made him comfortable and left him to get well, going on themselves up the river to get out a raft of saw-logs for Dawson. He was still limping slightly at the time he rescued Buck, but with the warming of the weather even the slight limp left him. And here, lying by the river bank through the long spring days, watching the running water, listening lazily to the songs of the birds and the hum of nature, he watched as Buck slowly won back his strength.

Buck, Thornton, and the dogs Skeet and Nig were waiting for the raft to come that was to carry them down to Dawson. Skeet was a little Irish setter who early on made friends with Buck. She had the doctor trait which some dogs possess, and as a mother cat washes her kittens, so she washed and cleansed Buck's wounds. Nig was a huge good-natured black dog, half bloodhound and half deerhound. To Buck's surprise these dogs were not jealous. They seemed as kind as Thornton. As Buck grew stronger, they got him involved in all sorts of play, and in this fashion Buck romped through his recovery and into a new life. Love was his for the first time. This he had never experienced at Judge Miller's in the sun-kissed Santa Clara Valley. With the Judge's sons and grandsons there had been friendship, but not this feeling. It had taken Thornton to draw out Buck's love.

through jutting rocks. Thornton knew that the shore was impossible. He was scraped over a rock, thrown against another and then another. He clutched the last rock with both hands, releasing Buck, and above the churning water shouted, "Go, Buck, go!"

Buck had been swept on downstream, struggling, but unable to get back to Thornton. When he heard Thornton's command repeated, he threw his head high, as though for a last look, and then turned toward the bank. He swam powerfully and was dragged ashore by Pete and Hans.

The men knew it was only a matter of minutes a man could cling to a slippery rock in the face of that driving current, and they ran as fast as they could up the bank to a point far above where Thornton was hanging on. They attached the line with which they had been holding onto the boat to Buck's neck and shoulders, being careful that it should neither strangle him nor slow his swimming, and carefully threw him into the stream. Buck struck out boldly, but not straight enough into the stream. He was carried past Thornton. Hans promptly reeled him in with the rope, as though Buck were a fish. The faint sound of Thornton's voice came to them, and though they could not make out the words, they knew he was in his last seconds. Buck sprang back into the water. He had miscalculated the first jump, but this time he got it right. Thornton saw him coming, and, as Buck swam into him like a battering ram, the man reached up and closed both arms around Buck's shaggy neck. Hans fastened the rope around a tree, and Buck and Thornton were jerked under the water for several moments. They were dragged over the jagged river bottom before reaching the bank.

Thornton and Buck were limp, seemingly dead, and Nig started to howl for his friends, while Skeet was licking their faces. Thornton was the first to gain his senses and rise up, and when he did, and saw Buck, who was hardly breathing, he petted and patted his furred friend until Buck, with a groan, woke as well. Thornton's heart almost burst with joy. Yet, when he discovered Buck had broken three ribs, he announced, "That settles it. We camp right here." And camp they did, till Buck's ribs healed and he was able to travel.

That winter, at Dawson, Buck performed another feat that earned him even more fame in Alaska. The feat was brought about by a conversation in the Eldorado Saloon, in which men boasted of their favorite dogs. Buck, because of his fame, was the target of teasing by these men, and Thornton was driven to defend him. At the end of half an hour one man stated that his dog could start a sled with five hundred pounds and walk off with it; a second bragged six hundred for his dog; and a third, seven hundred.

"Pooh!" said John Thornton. "Buck can start a thousand pounds."

"And break it out of the ice? And walk off with it for a hundred yards?" demanded Jervey Matthewson, a gold-mining king.

"And break it out, and walk off with it for a hundred yards," Thornton said.

"Well," Matthewson said, "I've got a thousand dollars that says he can't. And there it is." So saying, he slammed a sack of gold dust the size of a bologna sausage down upon the bar.

Nobody spoke. Thornton's boast had been challenged. But he did not know whether Buck could start a thousand pounds. A half a ton! He had great faith in Buck's strength and had often thought him capable of starting such a load; but never, as now, had he faced the possibility of it, the eyes of a dozen men upon him, silent and waiting. Further, he did not have a thousand dollars; nor had Hans or Pete.

"I've got a sled outside with twenty fifty-pound sacks of flour on it," Matthewson said, "so don't let that stop you from trying."

Thornton did not answer. He did not know what to say. He glanced from face to face. The face of Jim O'Brien, an old-time comrade, caught his eyes.

"Can you lend me a thousand?" he asked.

"Sure," answered O'Brien, thumping down a heavy sack of gold by the side of Matthewson's. "Though I doubt that your beast can do the trick, John," he said.

The men in the bar emptied out into the street to see the contest. The card-dealers came out as well to see the outcome and to take bets. Several hundred men, garbed in fur, surrounded the sled. Matthewson's sled, loaded with a thousand pounds of flour, had been standing for a couple of hours, and in the intense cold (it was sixty below zero) the runners had frozen to the hard-packed snow. Men offered odds of three to one that Buck could not budge the sled. But not a man was willing to place a bet on Buck. Now that Thornton had looked at the sled itself, it even seemed impossible to him.

Matthewson was happy enough to dance. "Three to one odds!" he laughed. "Thornton, I'll bet you another thousand at those odds. What d'ye say?"

Thornton's doubt was strong, but his anger at Matthewson's scoffing made him want to challenge the man. So he took the bet, but all he and Hans and Pete could come up with was six hundred dollars.

The team of ten dogs was unhitched, and Buck, with his own harness, was put into the sled. He was excited as well, and he felt he must do a great thing for Thornton. Many in the crowd admired the splendid dog. He was in perfect condition, without an ounce of extra fat, and his one hundred and fifty pounds were rock solid. Down the neck and across the shoulders, his hair half-bristled and seemed to lift with every movement. His huge chest and heavy forelegs were in proportion with the tight muscles of the rest of his body. Men felt these muscles and proclaimed them hard as iron, and the odds went down to two to one.

"Goll durn it, Thornton!" said the owner of the new gold-mine, "I offer you eight hundred dollars for him before the contest, sir; eight hundred just as he stands."

Thornton shook his head and stepped to Buck's side.

"You must stand off from him," protested Matthewson.

"Give him plenty of room, you."

The crowd fell silent; only the voices of the gamblers offering two to one could be heard. But no one would take the bet. Everybody saw that Buck was a magnificent animal, but twenty fifty-pound sacks of flour seemed too much for any dog to pull.

Thornton knelt down by Buck's side. He took the furry head in his two hands and rested his cheek on Buck's. He whispered in the dog's ear, "If you love me, Buck. If you love me." Buck whined with eagerness to do his master's bidding.

The crowd was watching. As Thornton got to his feet, Buck seized his master's hand softly between his jaws. It was his answer of yes and his declaration of love. Thornton smiled and stepped away.

"Now, Buck," he said.

Buck tightened the traces of the leather harness, then let them go slack. It was the way he had learned to gauge the weight of his load.

"Gee!" Thornton's voice rang out. This command meant "Go to the right!"

Buck swung to his right, and then made a plunging movement that jerked himself to a halt. The load quivered, and from under the iron runners of the sled arose a crisp crackling.

"Haw!" Thornton commanded.

Buck tried the same move, this time, as commanded, to the left. The crackling of the ice turned into a snapping, and the sled slightly turned and the runners slipped several inches. The sled was broken out. Men were holding their breaths.

"Now, *mush!*" called Thornton.

Buck threw himself forward, tightening the traces with a jarring lunge. His whole body was gathered together in the effort. His chest was low to the ground, his head forward and down, while his feet were flying like mad, the claws scarring the hard-packed snow in parallel grooves. The sled swayed and trembled, half-started forward. One of his feet slipped, and one man groaned aloud. Then the sled lurched ahead in what appeared to be a rapid series of jerks, though it really never came to a dead stop again ... half an inch ... an inch ... two inches ... The jerking seemed to vanish as the sled picked up speed and was moving steadily along.

Men gasped and began to breathe again. Thornton was running behind, encouraging Buck with short, cheery words. The distance had been measured off, and as he neared the pile of firewood which marked the end of the hundred yards, a cheer began to grow and grow, which burst into a roar as Buck passed the firewood and halted at command. Every man was hopping with glee, even Matthewson. Hats and mittens were flying in the air. Men were shaking hands and bubbling with amazement.

Thornton, for his part, fell on his knees beside Buck. He put his head against Buck's, and he shook the dog back and forth.

"Goll durn it, sir!" spluttered the gold mine king, "I'll give you a thousand dollars for him, sir—no, twelve hundred!"

Thornton rose to his feet. His eyes were wet with tears. "Sir," he said, "no, sir! Not for anything!"

6. The Sounding of the Call

WHEN BUCK earned twenty-eight hundred dollars in five minutes for John Thornton, he made it possible for his master to pay off many debts and to journey with his partners into the east after a lost mine that many had spoken of, but no one really knew about.

Thornton and Pete and Hans, with Buck and a half-dozen other dogs, set out to the east on an unknown trail. They sledded seventy miles up the Yukon, swung to the left into the Stewart River, passed the Dolly and the Carbotte, and held on until the Stewart itself became a tiny creek, threading the high mountains that marked the backbone of this continent.

Thornton was unafraid of the wild. With a handful of salt and a rifle he could plunge into the wilderness for as long as he pleased. He hunted his dinner in the course of a day's travel; and if he failed to find it, he kept on travelling, sure that sooner or later he would come to it.

To Buck this trip was a boundless delight, hunting, fishing, and wandering through strange places. For weeks at a time they would travel day after day; and for weeks upon end they would camp, here and there, the dogs loafing and the men burning holes through frozen muck and gravel and washing countless pans of dirt by the heat of the fire. Sometimes they went hungry, sometimes they feasted, all according to the luck of hunting. Summer arrived, and dogs and men packed off, rafting across mountain lakes and canoeing up or down rivers.

The months came and went, and back and forth the crew twisted through the unmapped north, where no men were and yet where men had been, if the stories of the gold mine were true. They went across ridges in summer blizzards, shivered under the midnight sun on bare mountains, dropped into summer valleys amid swarming gnats and flies, and in the shadows of glaciers picked strawberries and flowers. In the fall of the year they reached a strange lake country, where wildfowl had been, but where now there was no life nor sign of life—only the blowing of chilly winds, the forming of ice in sheltered places, and the sad rippling of waves on lonely beaches.

And through another winter they wandered on the broken trails of men who had gone before. Once, they came upon a path blazed through the forest, but the path began nowhere and ended nowhere, and it remained a mystery as to the man who made it and why he made it.

Spring came on once more, and at the end of all their wandering they found, not the lost goldmine, but a shallow gravel-bed in a broad valley where the gold showed like yellow butter across the bottom of a washing-pan. They decided to go no further. Each day they worked earned them thousands of dollars in dust and nuggets, and they worked every day. The gold was sacked in moose-hide bags, fifty pounds to a bag, and piled like so much firewood outside the spruce-bow lodge they had built.

There was nothing for the dogs to do but haul in the meat Thornton killed now and then, and Buck spent long hours musing by the fire.

But then there began the call from the depths of the forest. It filled Buck with unrest and strange desires. It caused him to feel an odd, sweet gladness, and he was aware of wild desires and stirrings for he didn't know what. Sometimes he followed the call into the forest, looking for it as though it was something he could see or touch or smell or taste. He would thrust his nose into the cool wood moss, or into the dark soil where long grasses grew, and snort with joy at the earthy smells; or he would crouch for hours, as if hiding, behind fungus-covered trunks of fallen trees, wide-eyed and wide-eared to all that moved and sounded about him. He did not know why he did these things. He felt he had to.

Strange needs came to him. He would be lying in camp, dozing lazily in the heat of the day, when suddenly his head would lift and his ears cock up, intent and listening, and he would spring to his feet and dash away, and on and on, for hours, through the forest lanes and across the open spaces. He loved to run down dry creek beds, and to creep and spy upon the bird life in the woods. For a day at a time he would lie in the underbrush where he could watch the partridges strutting up and down. But especially he loved to run in the dim twilight of the summer midnights, listening to the sleepy murmurs of the forest, reading signs and sounds as man may read a book, and seeking for a mysterious something that called and called, waking or sleeping, at all times, for him to come.

One night he sprang from sleep with a start, eager-eyed, nostrils quivering and sniffing, his hair bristling. From the forest came the call—a long-drawn howl, like, yet unlike, any noise made by a husky. And it seemed as if it was a sound he had heard before—beyond his own life. He sprang through the sleeping camp and in swift silence dashed through the woods. As he drew closer to the cry he went more slowly, with caution in every movement, till he came to an open place among the trees, and looking out saw, sitting up, with nose pointed to the sky, a long, lean timber wolf.

He had made no noise, yet it stopped its howling and became aware of Buck's presence. Buck stalked into the open, half-crouching, body gathered together, tail straight and stiff. Every movement he made seemed a combination of threat and friendliness, and the wolf fled at the sight of him. Buck followed, with wild leapings. He ran the wolf into a creek bed, where fallen timber barred the way. The wolf whirled about, pivoting on his hind legs, and snarled and bristled, clipping his teeth together in a series of snaps.

Buck did not attack, but circled about and hedged him in with friendly advances. The wolf was suspicious and afraid, for Buck was three times as heavy, while its head barely reached Buck's shoulder. Watching its chance, it darted away, and the chase was resumed. Time and again it was cornered by Buck, and the routine repeated, though it was in poor shape, or Buck could not so easily have overtaken him. It would run till Buck's head was even with its flank, when it would whirl around at bay, only to dash away again at the first opportunity.

But in the end Buck's persistence paid off; for the wolf, finding that no harm was intended, finally sniffed with him. Then they became friendly, and played about in a nervous, half-coy way. After some time of this the wolf started off at an easy lope in a manner that plainly showed he was going somewhere. He made it clear to Buck that he was to come, and they ran side by side

He made it clear to Buck that he was to come, and they ran side by side through the twilight.

through the twilight, straight up the creek bed, into the gorge from which it came, and across the ridge where it went further up.

On the opposite slope of the ridge they came down into a level country where there were great stretches of forest and many streams, and through these stretches they ran steadily, hour after hour, the sun rising higher and the day growing warmer. Buck was wildly glad. He knew he was at last answering the call, running by the side of his new brother toward the place from where the call surely came. Old memories were coming to him, as if he had run free in the open before.

They stopped by a running stream to drink, and, stopping, Buck remembered John Thornton. He sat down. The wolf started on toward the place from where the call surely came, then returned to Buck, sniffing noses and making actions as though to encourage him. But Buck turned about and started slowly backtracking. For the better part of an hour his wild brother ran by his side, whining. Then he sat down, pointed his nose upward, and howled. It was a mournful howl, and as Buck held steadily on his way he heard it grow faint and fainter until it was lost in the distance.

Thornton was eating dinner when Buck dashed into camp and sprang upon him with affection, licking his face and biting his hand.

For two days and nights Buck never left camp, never let Thornton out of his sight. He followed him about at his work, watched him while he ate, saw him into his blankets at night and out of them in the morning. But after two days the call in the forest began to sound more strongly than ever. Buck's restlessness came back to him, and he was haunted by the thought of his wild brother, and of the land beyond the ridge and the run through the wide forest. Once again he took to wandering in the woods, but the wild brother came no more; and though he listened for it, the mournful howl never came.

He began to sleep out at night, staying away from the

camp for days at a time; and once he crossed the ridge at the head of the creek and went down into the land of timber and streams. There he wandered for a week, seeking fresh signs of his brother, killing his meat as he travelled and travelling with the long, easy lope, never seeming to tire. He fished for salmon in a stream that emptied somewhere into the sea, and by this stream he killed a large black bear who blinded by the mosquitoes while likewise fishing, was raging through the forest helpless and terrible. Even so, it was a hard fight. And two days later, when Buck returned to his kill and found a dozen wolverines quarreling over the body, he scattered them, killing two.

He was becoming a killer, a beast that preyed in a hostile environment where only the strong survive. If not for the stray brown hairs on his muzzle, and above his eyes, and for the splash of white hair that ran down his chest, he might well have been mistaken for a giant wolf. From his St. Bernard father he had inherited size and weight, but it was his shepherd mother who had given shape to that size and weight. His muzzle was the long wolf muzzle, though it was larger than that of any wolf; and his head, somewhat broader, was the wolf head on a massive scale.

"Never was there such a dog," said Thornton one day, as the partners watched Buck marching out of the camp.

"When he was made, the mold was broke!" said Pete.

"Py jingo! I tink so mineself!" agreed Hans.

They saw him marching out of camp, but they did not see the instant and terrible transformation which took place as soon as he was within the secrecy of the forest. He no longer marched. At once he became a thing of the wild, stealing along softly, cat-footed, a passing shadow that appeared and disappeared among the shadows. He knew how to take advantage of every cover, to crawl on his belly like a snake, and like a snake to leap and strike. He could take a bird from its nest, kill a rabbit as it slept, and snap in midair the little chipmunks fleeing a second too late for the trees. Fish, in open pools, were not too quick for him; nor were beaver, mending their dams. He killed to eat, not for fun.

As the fall of the year came on, the moose appeared in greater numbers, moving slowly down to meet the winter in the lower and lusher valleys. Buck had already dragged down a stray part-grown calf; but he wished for larger and stronger prey. He came upon such moose one day on the ridge at the head of the creek. A band of twenty had crossed over from the land of streams and timber, and chief among them was a great bull. He was in a savage temper, and, standing over six feet from the ground, was as difficult an opponent as Buck could desire. Back and forth the bull tossed his great antlers. His small eyes burned while he roared at the sight of Buck.

In the bull's side, just in front of the flank, was stuck a feathered arrow-end. Guided by his instinct, Buck proceeded to cut the wounded bull out from the herd. It was no easy task. He would bark and dance about in front of the bull, staying just out of reach of the antlers and of the terrible hooves which could have stamped his skull in. Unable to turn its back on the fanged dog and go on, the bull would be driven into a rage. At such moments he charged Buck, who retreated, luring him on. But when the bull was separated from his fellows, two or three of the younger bulls would charge back on Buck and enable the wounded bull to rejoin the herd.

Buck was patient. He clung to the back of the herd, driving the bull mad with rage. For half a day this continued, with Buck attacking from all sides, wearing out the patience of the herd.

As the day wore along and the sun dropped to its bed in the northwest, the young bulls retraced their steps less often to come to the aid of their wounded leader. The winter was hurrying them forward, but it seemed they could not shake off this tireless creature that slowed them down.

As twilight fell the old bull stood with lowered head, watching his mates—the cows he had known, the calves

From that day on, day and night, Buck did not leave his prey.

he had fathered, the bulls he had mastered—as they shambled on at a rapid pace through the fading light. He could not follow, for before his nose leaped the merciless fanged terror that would not let him go. He weighed more than twelve-hundred pounds; he had lived a long, strong life full of fight and struggle, and at the end he faced death at the teeth of a creature whose head did not reach higher than his knuckled knees.

From then on, day and night, Buck did not leave his prey, never gave it a moment's rest, never permitted it to browse the leaves of trees or the shoots of young birch and willow. Nor did he give the wounded bull the chance to drink in the streams they crossed. Often, in desperation, the bull burst into long runs. At such times, Buck did not attempt to slow him down, but loped easily at his heels. When the moose stood still, Buck lay down, but attacked whenever it tried to eat or drink.

The moose's huge head drooped more and more under its tree of horns, and the shambling trot grew weaker and weaker. He took to standing for long periods, with nose to the ground and ears limp; and Buck found more time in which to get water for himself and in which to get rest. At such moments, panting with his tongue and eyes fixed upon the bull, it appeared to Buck that a change was coming over the face of things. He could feel a new stir in the land. As the moose were coming into the land, other kinds of life were also coming in. Forest and stream and air seemed to carry their presence. He would investigate after he had finished this business.

At long last, at the end of the fourth day, he pulled the moose down. For a day and a night he remained by the kill, eating and sleeping. Then, rested, refreshed and strong, he turned his face toward camp and John Thornton. He broke into his long easy lope, and went on, hour after hour, never at a loss through the tangled way, heading straight home through strange country.

As he held on he became more and more aware of the new stir in the land. There was a different life in it than had been there in the summer. The birds talked of it, the squirrels chattered about it. Several times he stopped and drew in the fresh morning air in great sniffs, reading a message which made him leap on with greater speed. He had a sense that something terrible had happened, and as he crossed the last ridge and dropped down into the valley toward camp he went on with caution.

Three miles away he came upon a fresh trail that sent his neck-hair rippling and bristling. It led straight to the camp and Thornton. Buck hurried on, swiftly, every nerve tense, alert to the many details which told a story—all but the end of the story. The bird-life had flitted. The squirrels were hiding.

As Buck slid along like a gliding shadow, his nose was jerked suddenly to the side with a new scent. He followed the smell and found Nig. He was lying on his side, dead where he had dragged himself, an arrow through his body.

A hundred yards farther on, Buck came upon one of the sled-dogs Thornton had bought in Dawson. This dog was dying, but Buck passed around him without stopping. From the camp came a faint sound of many voices, rising and falling in a sing-song chant. Bellying forward to the edge of the clearing, he found Hans, lying on his face, feathered with arrows like a porcupine. At the same instant Buck peered out where the spruce-bow lodge had been and saw what made his hair leap straight up on his neck and shoulders.

The Yeehat Indians were dancing about the wreckage of the lodge when they heard a fearful roaring and saw rushing upon them an animal the like of which they had never seen before. It was Buck, hurling upon them in a frenzy. He sprang at the first man (it was the chief), ripping the throat open. With the next bound he tore wide open the throat of a second man. The Indians understood that there was no fighting him. He plunged about in their midst, tearing through them; he moved so quickly that their arrows could not catch up to him. A panic seized the group, and they fled in terror to the woods, proclaiming that the Evil Spirit had come.

Buck chased after, raging at their heels and dragging them down like deer as they raced through the trees. It was a terrible day for the Yeehats. They scattered far and wide over the country, and it was not till a week later that the last of the survivors gathered together in a lower valley and counted their losses. As for Buck, he returned to the camp. He found Pete where he had been killed in his blankets in the first moment of surprise. Thornton's desperate struggle was written on the ground, and Buck scented every detail of it down to the edge of a deep pool. By the edge lay Skeet. The pool itself contained Thornton.

All day Buck brooded by the pool or roamed restlessly above the camp. Thornton's death left an emptiness in him, something like hunger, and it ached and ached. Night came on, and a full moon rose high over the trees into the sky, lighting the land till it lay bathed in ghostly day. And with the coming of the night, brooding by the pool, Buck became alive to a stirring of new life in the forest—a different sort of life from that of the men he had killed. He stood up, listening and scenting. From far away drifted a faint, sharp yelp, followed by a chorus of similar sharp yelps. As the moments passed the yelps grew closer and louder. Again Buck knew them as things heard from his dark memory. He walked to the center of the open space and listened. It was the call, the many-noted call, sounding more compelling than ever before. And as never before, he was ready to obey that call. Thornton was dead. Buck's last tie to life with mankind was broken.

Hunting their living meat, on the flanks of the migrating moose, as the Yeehats were hunting it, the wolf pack had at last crossed over from the land of streams and timber and invaded Buck's valley. Into the clearing where the moonlight streamed, they poured in a silvery flood; and in the center of the clearing stood Buck, motionless as a statue, waiting their coming. They were awed, he was so still and large, and there was a moment's pause before the boldest one leaped straight for him. Like a flash Buck struck, breaking the wolf's neck. Then he stood, without movement, as before. Three others tried it, and one after another they drew back, streaming blood from their necks or shoulders.

This brought the whole pack forward, eager to pull him down. Buck's marvellous quickness and agility allowed him to pivot on his hind legs, and, snapping and gashing, he was everywhere at once. But to prevent them from getting behind him, he was forced back, down past the pool and into a creek bed, till he was against a high gravel bank. He worked along to a right angle in the bank, which the men had made in the course of mining, and in this angle he came to bay, protected on three sides and with nothing to do but face the front.

And so well did he face it that at the end of half an hour, the wolves drew back. Their tongues were hanging, the fangs showing white in the moonlight. Some were lying down with heads raised and ears pricked forward; others stood on their feet, watching him; and still others were lapping water from the pool. One wolf, long and lean and gray, advanced cautiously, in a friendly manner, and Buck recognized the wild brother with whom he had run for a night and a day. He was whining softly, and, as Buck whined, they touched noses.

Then an old wolf, thin and battle-scarred, came forward. Buck sniffed with him as well. The old wolf then sat down, pointed nose at the moon, and broke out the long wolf howl. The others sat down and howled. And now the call came to Buck. He, too, sat down and howled. This over, he came out of his angle and the pack crowded around him, sniffing in half-friendly, half-savage manner. The leaders lifted the yelp of the pack and sprang away

The Yeehats tell of a Ghost Dog that runs at the head of the pack.

into the woods. The wolves swung in behind, yelping in chorus. And Buck ran with them, side by side with his wild brother, yelping as he ran.

And here may well end the story of Buck. It was not many years before the Yeehats noted a change in the breed of timber wolves; for some were seen with splashes of brown on head and muzzle, and with a rift of white down the chest. But more remarkable than this, the Yeehats tell of a Ghost Dog that runs at the head of the pack. They are afraid of this Ghost Dog, for it has cunning, stealing from their camps in fierce winters, robbing their traps, slaying their dogs and defying their bravest hunters. Each fall, when the Yeehats follow the movement of the moose, there is a certain valley which they never enter.

In the summers, however, there is one visitor to that valley. It is a great wolf, like yet unlike all other wolves. He crosses alone from the timber land and comes down into an open space among the trees. Here a yellow stream flows from rotted moose-hide sacks and sinks into the ground, with long grasses growing through it and hiding its yellow from the sun. And here Buck muses for a time, howling once, long and mournfully, before he leaves.

But he is not always alone. When the long winter nights come on and the wolves follow their meat into the lower valleys, he may be seen running at the head of the pack through the pale moonlight, a giant among his fellows, his throat bellowing as he sings a song of the old world, the song of the pack.